Hooves of Fire

Minnie & Moo
HOOVES OF FIRE

Written and illustrated by Denys Cazet

Published by Creston Books, LLC
www.crestonbooks.co

Library of Congress Catalog Number 2013038846

Source of Production: Worzalla Books, Stevens Point, Wisconsin
Printed and bound in the United States of America
1 2 3 4 5

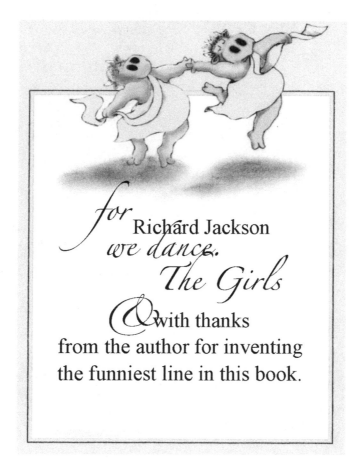

for Richard Jackson
we dance.
          The Girls

&with thanks
from the author for inventing
the funniest line in this book.

A letter from Minnie

A letter from Minnie

Dear Reader,

When my best friend, Moo, came up with the idea for a talent festival on our farm, I considered it one of the worst ideas I'd ever heard in my life.

And I mean ever, even from Moo.

She called it The First Annual Hoot, Holler, Cluck, Howl, Roar, Honk, Chirp, Bark, Meow, Whinny, Neigh, Bray, Oink, Grunt, Quack Minnie and Moo Poetry, Song, and Dance Red Tractor Farm Talent Festival of the Ages.

She asked my opinion.

I told her.

But I didn't say anything in a mean way.

You know how it is when your best friend does or says something you think is silly and then they ask you what you think. Because you love them so much, you can't say, "Are you nuts? That idea is dumber than licking an electric light socket!" No, you can't say it that way. You have to say you don't like it or you don't agree in a way that won't make them mad (or in Moo's case, hurt her feelings). After all, it's what good friends do. So what I said was, "Moo, the title is too long."

And that was that.

Almost.

Sincerely,

Minnie

1

Welcome

It was Indian summer on the farm.

The air smelled of damp leaves and fallen apples. An autumn breeze wandered aimlessly up the hill and settled in the limbs of the old oak tree where Minnie and Moo stood on a wooden stage.

They watched all the animals gathering below them at the foot of the hill. Some had spread out blankets on the grass for an afternoon picnic, while others milled about waving to old friends or stopping to be introduced to new ones.

Most of the animals were from neighboring farms. But some, like Irene, the rhinoceros, had once lived in the city zoo. Now she lived on Red Tractor Farm with Minnie and Moo. If Mr. and Mrs. Farmer noticed Irene, they hadn't mentioned it. There were even a few animals from Africa World who had taken their vacations early to help Minnie and Moo get ready for the festivities. Moo waved to Irene. Irene returned the wave and then went back to handing out the music to the band.

Minnie stood in the center of the stage watching Nadine, the water buffalo, filling the shelves of the Pastry Booth. Two coyotes walked by. When Nadine wasn't looking, they snatched half a dozen pastries and didn't pay for them.

"Ah," sighed Moo. "Look at that blue sky. A perfect day for the First Annual Hoot, Holler, and Moo Talent Festival."

"Maybe," grumbled Minnie, adjusting Moo's toga. "I just hope the farmer doesn't come home early from his vacation! There's always something that can go wrong. Look at those coyotes in black jackets. They just stole some pastries, raspberry, I think. And they rode in on motorcycles! Can you believe it? Motorcycles! And the weasels, see, look how close to the chickens they're sitting, and..."

"You worry too much, Minnie. We have security, see, over there, the Boarzinni brothers, Big Vinnie and Little Vinnie. They're professional hog wrestlers. So stop worrying."

Moo plugged in the microphone.

"It's my job to worry! You think. I sneeze. We're cows! We should all be walking around on four legs and eating grass!"

"Minnie! When was the last time you ate any grass?"

"That's not the point!"

"Last night," said Moo, tapping on the microphone, "you had Linguine Parmigiana, a Caesar salad, two banana splits, and a chocolate milkshake. For breakfast you had three cream puffs, two chocolate éclairs, and an extra large Hershey bar!"

"No nuts," said Minnie.

"What?"

"It was just a plain Hershey bar!"

Moo smiled. She put her arm around her best friend. "Try not to worry."

"I can't help it, Moo. Thinking leads to worry! When you start thinking, I start sneezing. My face gets all scrunched up. My mascara runs. And look, I'm getting crow's feet." Minnie leaned her face closer to Moo. "See?"

Moo looked at Minnie's feet. "I don't see any crow's feet. They look like hooves to me."

"Not down there! Up here, my eyes, see, wrinkles, worry lines, crow's feet."

Moo shrugged and then raised the microphone. "I can't help thinking. Sometimes I just think. I wonder about things. I just do."

Minnie sneezed. "I know."

"We're doing this for the best of reasons," said Moo. "Everyone has talent and should have an opportunity to express it. Look at all the money we've earned so far from ticket sales. It's going to a good cause. It will be fun."

Minnie saw two weasels next to the judges' table.

"Hey!" she yelled. "What are you doing?"

"What?" said the bigger weasel.

"You heard me!"

"Is that the money box?" asked the smaller weasel. His eyes seemed to shine as he stared at the metal box. Minnie snatched it up.

"None of your business," she snarled.

"Be a shame," said the larger weasel, still staring at the box, "to lose all that money. What with the good cause it would be goin' to and all."

"Shame," repeated the smaller weasel. "All those good animals working so hard." He shook his head sadly. "Shame."

"Shame," said the other weasel. They walked away. The smaller weasel whispered something to the bigger one and they both looked back and laughed.

"Trouble," muttered Minnie.

"Minnie!" Moo shouted from the middle of the stage. "Irene has all the band members on stage. They're ready to start."

"There must be a hundred animals out there," Minnie said, walking over to Moo. "How many did you invite?"

"I invited everyone."

"Moo, I see trouble. We should cancel. Two weasels were just…"

"Minnie, will you relax! Little Vinnie and Big Vinnie will be wandering around. They'll keep an eye out for trouble. Besides, it's too late to cancel. Everyone has worked too hard. Look at the program. It's full of original work… poems, songs, music, dance, magic, all from the heart. Don Juan del Toro has written something, a romantic poem. Bea and Madge Holstein will be reciting, Porkus Hockus will be singing the blues, and the Poulettes will be dancing. Even Zeke and Zack will be doing something. We can't let them all down."

"Zeke and Zack? The Siamese turkeys joined at the beak?"

"They're not joined anymore. Not since the accident."

Just as Minnie started to ask something else, a loud drum roll and cymbals crashed behind her.

"The band is ready," said Moo. "Testing, testing. Which is better, to be or not to be, a bee in Auntie Bea's bonnet or a hot cross bun in her bloomers? That is the question."

Irene nodded and the band started to play

softly in the background.

Minnie stared at Moo.

"What?"

"Moo, did you make that up about the bee in Auntie Bea's bonnet?"

"I got it from Shakespeare," said Moo.

"William Shakespeare?"

"No, Ed Shakespeare…William's brother."

"Well, I hope Ed is doing something useful with his life besides writing about his auntie's bloomers!"

Minnie sat down at the judges' table.

"Look for yourself," Moo suggested. "The Shakespeare book is on the table."

Minnie picked up the book and paged through it.

Moo raised her arms and shouted into the microphone. "WELCOME!"

The crowd applauded wildly as they found their places and sat down.

Minnie stared at the book. "Moo!"

"What?"

"This book is in Chinese!"

2

No Meat Will Be Served

The microphone squealed and Moo stepped back a little. "Thank you and welcome to the First Annual Hoot, Holler, and Moo Talent Festival.

"I have a few announcements. Your judges today will be myself and Minnie. Scores will be based on whim, impulse, and passing fancy. Scores will range from a low of one to a high of ten. Prizes will be awarded at the end of the Festival.

"All proceeds will be donated to Mr. and Mrs. Farmer for the down payment on a new tractor. We all remember what happened to the old one."

Minnie raised an eyebrow at the memory.

"No meat will be served at the snack bar. Please turn off your cell phones. The port-a-potties are parked at the top of the hill. Do not remove the blocks from under the wheels."

There was a murmur from the weasels.

"Trouble," Minnie muttered.

"And now, let the festival begin!" Moo shouted. "Ladies and gentlemen! Let's give a warm welcome to our first talents of the day, Zeke and Zack, reciting an original turkey poem, sung in two-part harmony and…"

Suddenly a rooster, dressed in a white luminescent jumpsuit with sequins and a cape, pushed past Zeke and Zack. His top feathers were combed back and held together with a heavy hair gel. He grabbed the microphone.

"Good afternoon, ladies and germs. You all know me. I'm Elvis, the rooster with the voice that's so melodious, it makes the sun come up every morning for each and every one of you lovely, lovely animals. First…"

"Hey!" demanded Zeke.
"We're first!"

Elvis smiled. "No, you're not. Look at the program."

Minnie carried over a program and showed it to Moo.

"Now what?"

Minnie pointed to the talent list. Someone had crossed off "Zeke and Zack" and written in "Elvis." Elvis smiled.

There was a murmur from the audience as they waited for the show to begin.

"Hey!" One of the weasels shouted. "Get on with the show or give us our money back."

Moo could see the coyotes and the weasels roaming around the audience, making comments. Two of the weasels were trying to sell cigars to a group of young sheep.

Minnie noticed it, too. "Get off the stage," she hissed at Elvis.

Elvis folded his wings dramatically. "My turn! Look at the program."

The coyotes began stomping their feet. "Money back! Money back! Money back!" they chanted. The Boarzinnis walked toward them.

"Zeke and Zack," said Moo nervously. "Would you mind switching places with Elvis?"

Minnie glared at Elvis. "Why don't I just toss him into the front row and…"

"Minnie, please, you're not helping."

The audience grew louder.

Zeke and Zack shrugged and walked off.

"Thank you," said Moo. She pulled Minnie back to the judges' stand. The audience quieted down as Elvis stepped up to the microphone again. There was a smattering of applause.

"The little twerp," Minnie grumbled. "I'm going to give Zeke and Zack an extra point."

"Thank you for that warm welcome," cooed Elvis. "I'd like to take a moment to thank the good people who put all this together, the judges, my closest friends, Vinnie and Lou."

Elvis pointed at Minnie and Moo. The audience applauded again, wondering who he was talking about.

Moo looked at Minnie. "Vinnie?"

"Lou?"

Elvis made a sweeping gesture toward a group of chickens in glittering dresses behind him. "The Poulette Supremos!"
he shouted.

The chickens giggled as the crowd cheered and whistled. They waved at the audience.

"Whoo, whoo," howled a coyote.

"Now you're talking!" said another.

"How about coming over for dinner!" yelled a weasel. "Bring a couple of friends! We'll bring the gravy!"

"I just knew they were going to be trouble," said Minnie.

Little Vinnie walked down one side of the crowd while Big Vinnie walked down the other. They glared at the coyotes.

Elvis pointed at the band. "And let's hear it for the beautiful Irene, the hippopotamus! Lookin' good, sweetheart. Have you lost a little weight?"

"Rhinoceros," said Minnie.

"What?"

"Rhinoceros. Irene is a rhinoceros, not a hippo."

"Rhino, hippo, what's the difference? When you're that big, you can be anything you want. She's fatter than a cow, and that's saying something!"

"That's it!" Minnie jumped up and stomped across the stage toward Elvis.

Moo grabbed Minnie and tried to calm her down. "Minnie, that's not going to do any good."

"It'll do *me* some good!"

"I know. Please sit down."

"I don't like fat jokes!"

"Do you mind?" asked Elvis. "I'm trying to warm up the crowd."

Minnie rolled her eyes. "*You* couldn't heat up this crowd with a blow torch!"

3

Eggs

Minnie glared at the rooster.

Elvis lowered the microphone. "As I was saying before I was so rudely interrupted, I'd like to thank Irene the Whatever, leader of our wonderful band. I'd also like to thank myself for writing this fabulous song I call *Because Of Me*, and again, thanks to our judges, my good friends, Ninny and Sue."

Minnie started to say something but was drowned out by the band as Elvis began singing.

Ohhhhhhhhhhhh…
I'm the Cocka Doodle Dandy
That doodles up the sun.
No one starts the day
Till I say it's all begun.
I cocka doodle once,
I cocka doodle twice,
I cocka doodle, cocka doodle,
Cocka doodle thrice!
I'm the Cocka Doodle Dandy,
As every chick can see.
I'm as handsome as they come,
I know you all agree.
I'm the Cocka Doodle Dandy
That doodles up the sun.
The Cocka Doodle Dandy
That doodles up the sun.

"Ahh, thank you," crowed the rooster. "And now, you wonderful audience, you're in for a special treat: ME, singing *My Way!*"

"Your way?" someone shouted. "Your way is the highway...bring on the girls!"

"Yeah," someone else shouted. "The girls!"

Soon the crowd was chanting, "The girls, the girls, we want the girls!"

"Okay, okay," grumbled Elvis. "What do these peasants know about talent? Girls, do you have a song?"

"All we know are cheers," said a chicken named Balinda.

"Cheers?"

"You know, chicken cheers, hen house cheers, motivational cheers...like for Meg, when she gets a little bound up."

"THE GIRLS!" shouted the crowd.

Elvis put the microphone on its stand. "Hurry up, girls. They're getting mean out there!"

The Poulettes gathered around the microphone with Meg in the middle. Several of the chickens passed out red and blue pom poms.

"Ready, girls?" shouted Zinnia. "GO!"

Sis Boom Bah!
Rah! Rah! Rah!
Come on, Meg,
Lay that egg!
You can do it!
You can do it!
You can do it NOW!
You can do it!
You can do it!
You can do it HOW?
Push, Push

puuusssssssssssssssHHH

"Let's hear it for my girls!" yelled Elvis. He bounced onto the middle of the stage and snatched the microphone. "Aren't they wonderful, folks? And now for something really wonderful, my version of...OH!"

Eggs covered the floor. Broken eggs stuck to Elvis's blue suede shoes. "Girls, girls, girls," he stammered. "What happened here?"

"We were motivated!"

"Geeze Louize, girls! Your timing is a little off. How about a smidge of self-control? Couldn't you hold it until I got off the stage? Couldn't you use precautions? And what's that?" he asked, pointing to an egg about the size of a marble.

"I laid that," Meg mumbled.

"Geeze," said Elvis. "I've seen bigger eggs in a hummingbird's nest!"

"OH!" wailed Meg. "Nothing's ever good enough for you, is it?"

"Come on, ladies," ordered Zinnia, leading the Poulettes away.

"Girls, come back! I haven't done *All Of Me* yet!"

"We've all had enough of you," said another chicken, as they fluttered off the stage. "Do you think the sun rises and sets just for you?"

"Well, yeah," said Elvis thoughtfully.

4

The "P" Word

Zeke and Zack waddled back on the stage.

Zeke stuck out his tongue at Elvis.

Elvis looked at the judges' table. "I'm not done here," he said, holding the microphone behind his back. "Fair is fair!"

"Everyone gets a chance," said Moo. "It's their turn."

"That's fair!" said Minnie. "You should have learned that in kindergarten!"

Zack grabbed the microphone.

"What are you doing? I'm not finished! I've got a squillion songs. This crowd worships me."

"Our turn," said Zeke and Zack.

"Look, fellas," whispered Elvis. "I'm on a roll here. They love me. Give me the microphone. I'll be done in a couple of hours."

"Our turn!"

Elvis slapped his forehead. "Geeze Louize," he moaned, looking over at Minnie and Moo. "Don't these birds need to get ready for Thanksgiving or something? You're the judges, can't you take care of this?"

Minnie shrugged. "Sure. Get off the stage!"

"Okay, okay," complained Elvis, covering the microphone. "But cut it short. I'm doing *My Way* next, followed by *I Gotta Be Me*."

Zeke and Zack stared straight ahead as they recited their poem.

My name is Zeke.

              My name is Zack.

We are turkeys.

              Think of that!

We eat a little here.

              We poop a little there.

Eat a little, poop a little, poo poo everywhere.

33

"Oh!" Minnie gasped.
"That was the most disgusting
thing I've ever heard uttered
in public!"

"I'm giving them an extra point for sinceri-ty," said Moo.

"There's no sincerity in the 'double p' word," Minnie exclaimed. She erased the extra point.

34

Zeke and Zack handed Elvis the microphone and walked off the stage.

The audience was silent.

"Sorry about that, folks," said Elvis. "That's why they call them turkeys. Bricks have bigger brains than they do. I've seen fence posts smarter than them birds." Elvis laughed. "But seriously, friends, I'm such a lucky guy. I'm the last person I see in the evening before I go to sleep and the first person I see when I wake up...so, I thought I'd change the menu a little and sing one of my favorites and yours, too, *Lucky Ol' Me* and..."

A loud slurping noise interrupted Elvis. It sounded like someone pulling off a rubber glove.

"What the, the..."

Moo walked over to the microphone.

"Thank goodness! You finally made it!"

"Made it?" asked the rooster.

"Not you. Him!"

Elvis peered closely at a moving bump on the microphone. "That's a snail!" he protested. "I'm supposed to give up my spot for a glob of snot on a half shell?"

Minnie stood up and walked over to Elvis. She pointed to the program. "Snail is next!"

"But I'm not finished!"

Minnie glared at the rooster. "And now a poem by Snail," she announced.

"Slug with a carport," Elvis whined.

"My poem," said Snail in a tiny voice, "is called *Wisdom of the Gastropoda.*"

Take it easy,
Take it slow,
The more you listen,
The more you know.

"That's good advice for everyone," Minnie agreed, looking at Elvis. "Do you have another?"

"No time," said Snail. "I've got to rush back. I'm helping a friend write a book about a snail that plays baseball."

"Here," said Minnie, picking up Snail. "I'll carry you back to the garden."

37

"Oh, thank you. That will save me about six weeks of traveling time!"

"Now may I continue?" asked Elvis.

"No! Don Juan del Toro is next."

"That big lug! What's he got that I haven't got?"

"Horns! Get off the stage."

"Ha! Can Mr. Horns do this?" Elvis began flapping his wings, dancing, until he slipped and fell off the stage with a squawk. Don Juan, who was waiting to be introduced, picked Elvis up. The audience applauded.

"Very funny," sneered Elvis. "It's a good thing I'm taking a potty break."

5

Hooves Of Fire

Moo got up and adjusted the microphone. She nodded toward Irene, and Irene pointed at a Gorilla named Moe, the band's drummer. The drums rolled and the cymbals crashed.

"Thank you, ladies and gentlemen, and now back to our presentation with our next talent, Don Juan del Toro!"

The audience hooted and hollered as Don Juan strode confidently across the stage while the band played the theme from Rocky. His chest was thrust out and his head held high, his muscles glistening in the sun. He stopped in front of the microphone and gave the audience a polite bow and cleared his throat.

"Handsome devil," said Minnie. "And he knows it, too!"

"And strong," added Moo, sitting down. "I once saw him crush a rusty root beer can against his forehead. He smashed it! Wham! He didn't even flinch!"

Minnie raised her eyebrows.

"...and those long horns," Moo sighed.

"Moo. This is a talent contest...not a beauty contest!"

"I am Don Juan del Toro," declared Don Juan. He flexed his biceps and the crowd gasped.

"Whoa," whispered Moo, fanning herself. "If that isn't a 10, I don't know what is!"

"My poem," announced Don Juan.

I am Don Juan del Toro
From old sunny Mexico.
Watch my muscles ripple
As I flex from head to toe.
When I stride across the pasture,
I hear cries of "Magnifico!"
I cannot pass a herd of cows
Without…"Bravissimo!"
Even though I know
I can whip the buffalo,
My heart becomes as gentle as the dove
Beneath the mistletoe.
For when I gaze upon your face,
My eyes see nothing but a rainbow,
Blinding the memory of loves lost
In old sunny Mexico.

The audience applauded as Don Juan laid a long-stemmed rose on the judges' table in front of Moo. He leaned over and whispered in Moo's ear.

"And now I, Don Juan del Toro, will dance with you. The sun shall bear witness to my love. Do not be afraid, my little milk bucket."

Moo gulped as Don Juan del Toro strode proudly to the center of the stage. "Music, please."

Nadine blew a Spanish trumpet powerfully and melodically into the blue, cloudless sky. It echoed across the hills as Don Juan turned slowly and reached out dramatically to Moo.

"We shall dance the *Hooves of Fire!*"

Moo tightened up her toga.

Minnie handed Moo her castanets and flamenco shoes. "The big galoot. Show him how it's done, Moo!"

Moo got up and took a deep breath.

She threw her head back and raised
her arms above her head. She clacked
the castanets slowly as she swayed
toward Don Juan.

The band matched the tempo of Moo's steps. She danced around Don Juan, quickening her pace. Soon they were both dancing around each other. Moo began stomping the floor. She twirled around and around, and then, suddenly, she stopped, threw her arms back, and stared at Don Juan with such ferocity he began to sweat.

"Olé!" shouted the crowd.

Again, Moo began to slowly tap, tap to the rhythm of the music, hoofing it around and around Don Juan, and again, suddenly, pounded the floor as she threw up her arms, clacked her castanets, and glared at him until he felt weak in the knees. He tried to keep up, but finally danced off the stage as gracefully and as honorably as he could muster.

"Olé!" shouted the audience.

"Olé!" shouted Minnie.

Moo limped over and sat down next to Minnie. Slowly she slid under the table. Breathing heavily, she reached out to Minnie.

"Olé!" she whimpered. "Isn't he something?"

"What's wrong with you?" Minnie said, slapping Moo's wrist.

"He is magnifico!" Moo whispered.

Minnie put a cold, damp cloth on Moo's forehead. "MEDIC!" she yelled as she fanned Moo's face with her scorecard.

"Bravissimo!" Moo sighed weakly.

An old goat in a white coat pushed his way through the crowd that had gathered at the foot of the stage. He set his black bag down next to Moo.

"What seems to be the trouble?"

"Her radiator is overheated," said Minnie.

The doctor frowned. "What?"

Moo reached up and gently touched Minnie.

"Promise me that when I cross to the great pasture in the sky, you'll bury me in my favorite sequined red dress, and, and..."

"...and what?"

Moo looked sadly at Minnie. "...and I'd like to be holding my castanets."

"Moo, get up! Everyone is staring at us."

The doctor closed up his bag. "Fever!" he announced and walked off the stage.

49

Moo smiled weakly. "Gracias."

She picked up her scorecard and wrote a 15 after Don Juan del Toro's name.

"Moo, the highest score is a 10. How can you give someone a 15, if the highest score possible is 10?"

Moo picked up the rose and inhaled deeply. "Minnie, don't you see? Didn't you feel the Latin depths of Don Juan's tribute to love...the passion, the fire, the..."

"Fever," finished Minnie.

"Yes!"

"So love is like getting the flu."

"No," cried Moo. "It's like this rose. See, Don Juan even removed the thorns."

Minnie shrugged. "What's love without a few thorns?"

"Perfecto."

Moo picked up the rose, inhaled its rich, sweet fragrance, and stared at the empty stage.

"Wonderful, don't you think?"

Minnie didn't answer.

Moo looked around the stage. Minnie was gone. And worse, so was the money box.

6

Race Of The Port-A-Potties

Moo stood up and searched the crowd for Minnie. "Now what?" she muttered as she crossed the stage. "Ladies and gentlemen," she announced, "there will be a brief intermission."

Moo switched off the microphone and walked over to the bandstand. "Break time," she told the band leader.

"Fifteen minutes," said Irene.

The band wandered off toward the cold drink stand, grumbling about short breaks.

"You look worried," said Irene.

Moo nodded. "Have you seen Minnie?"

"I just saw her." Irene looked out across the milling crowd. "Isn't that her in front of the ice cream booth?"

"I can't tell."

"Why? What's the matter?"

"The money box is missing."

"She probably took it with her."

Moo fussed with her toga. "I hope so…the weasels were hanging around!"

"Uh oh."

Moo and Irene worked their way through the crowd and stopped at the ice cream booth.

Minnie wasn't there.

"What can I get you?" asked a small pig named Hamlet.

"We're looking for Minnie," said Irene.

"She was just here. She ordered a triple tall chocolate shake, laced with a double shot of mocha, extra whip."

"Was she carrying anything?" Moo asked.

"Well, yeah! That's a tall order."

"No, I mean like a tin box with a lock on it."

"Maybe." Hamlet shrugged. "It's been busy."

"Did you see which way she went?"

"Up." Hamlet pointed toward the six port-a-potties at the top of the hill.

"Maybe we'd better wait here," said Irene. "She should come down any minute."

Moo glanced over at the bottom of the hill.

Irene squinted in the direction Moo was looking. The hyenas, the coyotes, and the weasels were stretching a ribbon from one side to the other.

One of the hyenas held up a checkered flag.

"I don't like the looks of this," said Moo.

The port-a-potties began rocking back and forth and then slowly rolling down the hill.

When the crowd realized the port-a-potties were headed straight toward them, they pushed and shoved each other to get out of the way.

There were caws and quacks and baas and muffled shouts from inside the six potties as they rolled faster and faster down the hill. One potty hit a rock and bounced into another.

The doors popped open, and a sheep flew out of one and a rooster tumbled out of the other.

Faster and faster the potties sped, scattering the crowd right and left as they raced to the bottom of the hill and across the finish line, the broken ribbon twirling into the air.

The checkered flag came down and pointed at the farthest potty, which had rolled to a stop in front of the pastry booth.

"Number three!" shouted one of the coyotes. "A winner at 10-to-1 odds. Second place, number one, and third to show, at 6-to-1 odds, potty number six. Please see Slick for all bets."

The door to potty number three opened and Minnie stumbled out, holding an empty milk shake container.

"What happened? One minute I'm sitting there, minding my own business, and the next I'm covered in milk shake with a straw up my nose!"

"Are you okay?" Moo asked.

"I think so. Where's the money box?"

"You don't have it?"

"I thought I did!"

The Boarzinni brothers pushed their way

through the crowd. "Somebody, or somebodies, pushed those potties down the hill," said Little Vinnie. He looked over at the coyotes.

"We've lost the money box!" Moo wailed.

Big Vinnie stared at the weasels and hyenas talking and laughing with each other. A red fox by the name of Slick was holding a wad of money.

"I'm going to check something out," he said.

Moo and Irene followed the two brothers. Nadine found a damp towel and helped Minnie clean up. She gave her a fresh toga.

Little Vinnie nodded at the fox. "Howdy," he said. "Making a little money?"

Slick looked up and smiled. "All for a good cause."

"Yours or ours?"

"What business is it of yours?" asked one of the coyotes.

Slick held up his hand. "Now, now, we're all friends here. Yours, of course."

"Yeah, sure!" snickered one of the hyenas.

One of the coyotes started to back away.

"What's that behind your back?" Little Vinnie asked.

"Show them," ordered Slick.

The coyote held up the box.

"Hooray!" Moo cheered. "You found it!"

"Absolutely," said Slick. "Tyrone, give Miss Moo the money box we found and saved for her, so no unscrupulous characters would try to steal it and ruin this great charity event."

Big Vinnie stared hard at the fox.

"And here's the money we made on our surprise racing event," added Slick. "Our donation."

"Wow!" said Moo. "That's very generous."

"A little too generous," mumbled a weasel.

60

Slick watched the Boarzinni brothers, Irene, and Moo as they walked away.

"What did you do that for?" whispered one of the coyotes.

"Shut up," snarled Slick. "There's more than one way to skin a cow."

"What do you mean?"

"Did you get the stuff I asked for?"

Two of the weasels nodded.

Slick smiled. "Patience. Our turn's coming."

Minnie met everyone at the Pastry Booth. "Did you find the money box?"

"Yes, and we made some extra money from the potty races, even though they weren't on our schedule," said Moo cheerfully. "It's nice when others surprise you with good works. The coyotes were very generous. They're not so bad after all."

"Yeah, right," said Minnie, staring at the weasels. "You try bouncing down a hill at a hundred miles an hour. I lost an unfinished milk shake! That really burns me up! They're up to something, Moo."

"I don't trust them, either," growled Little Vinnie. "If they're so trustworthy, why was that coyote hiding the money box behind his back?"

"Maybe he was just waiting to give it back," said Moo. "Maybe he just wanted to surprise us. A surprise gift for the festival."

"That ride down the hill in a port-a-potty wasn't a gift," Minnie complained. "A surprise, yes…a gift, no!"

Irene pointed toward the stage. "Let's get back. The band is waiting."

"Go ahead," Minnie mumbled, looking at the pastry sign above her. "A ride like that can work up a girl's appetite."

"What'll you have?" asked Nadine, leaning across the counter.

"I'll have six éclairs, a dozen cream puffs, and two Danishes to go, please."

7

My Mother Was A Holstein

When the audience saw Minnie, Moo, and Irene crossing the stage, they settled back into their places. Moo and Minnie returned to the judges' table. The Boarzinni brothers directed the coyotes and hyenas as they dragged the port-a-potties back up the hill and replaced the blocks under the wheels.

"Where's the money box?" Moo asked.

"I'm sitting on it," said Minnie, polishing off a cream puff.

"Well, don't let it out of your sight!"

"Moo, I'm sitting on it. Just because I can't see it, doesn't mean I don't know where it is!"

"Okay, okay…who's next?"

"Bea and Madge Holstein…"

A horrid, squealing racket exploded across the hillside. The audience covered their ears and tried to hide behind each other. Some threw blankets over their heads and cried for help. The shrill, piercing noise sounded like a pig caught in a revolving door.

"OW!" cried Minnie.

"It's Elvis!" yelled Moo. "He's playing the bagpipes!"

"What?"

"Bagpipes!" shouted Moo.

"My head! Make him stop!"

Moo jumped up and turned off the amplifier.

The sound went dead. The audience fell back on the grass, gasping.

"What happened?" Elvis tapped on the dead microphone. "What's the matter with this thing? It's not working."

Minnie stood up and waved Elvis away. "Get off the stage. It's not your turn."

"What are you talking about?" asked Elvis, pointing at the audience. "They loved it. Look at them. They're lying on the grass, soaked in joy!"

"That's pain!" cried Minnie. "They're soaked in pain. Get off the stage!"

Bea and Madge Holstein stood behind Elvis.

"You heard her!" said Madge. "Off!"

"Okay, okay! But you'll be sorry. You don't know what you're missing! I was going to play *Love Is A Many Splendid Thing* on a rubber band!"

"I'm sorry we'll miss it," said Bea. "Off!"

"Cows," Elvis mumbled as he dragged the squeaking bagpipes off the stage.

Moo flipped on the sound system.

"And now," she announced, "for our next act, Bea and Madge Holstein reciting original works of poetry."

Only half the audience applauded. The rest

were waiting in line at the First Aid booth, hoping for a cup of water and free aspirin.

Moo sat down next to Minnie.

"At last," said Minnie, eating another éclair. "The Holsteins have been working on this for months. I'm sure it's wonderful. I think I'll give them a 10."

"Minnie, you can't give them a score before you've even heard the poem."

"Moo, Madge told me it's about cows. It must be good."

"Minnie..."

"Moo...you were the one who wanted to give Don Juan del Muscles a score of 15."

Moo blushed. "I was confused!"

"Oh, all right," said Minnie. "I'll wait until they're done. Then I'll give them a 10."

Madge sprayed her throat with freshener.

"Mee, mee, mee."

"It's always about you, you, you!"

"What?"

"You, you, you!" repeated Bea.

"What's wrong with you?" whispered Madge. "We're on stage, Bea. Everyone is staring at us. I was just loosening up my throat!"

"I want to be first," said Bea. "I have a song."

Madge shook her head. "I was wondering why you were wearing tap dancing shoes and carrying that cane." Madge stepped back. "Be my guest. The stage is yours."

Bea pointed the cane at the band and they struck up a quick tune. She tap danced across the stage and sang her new song:

> *My mother was a Holstein*
> *On a dairy farm.*
> *They milked her every day*
> *In the dairy barn.*

> *It seems so very sad to me,*
> *It ought to be a crime…*
> *For all the milk she gave away,*
> *She never got a dime.*

Bea fell on one knee and shouted: "Good evening, friends!" The audience cheered.

"Finished?" Madge asked.

"I have one more."

Madge glared at her sister.

"It's short."

"Why didn't you tell me about this before we got on stage?"

Bea shrugged.

"What's it about?"

"Cows."

"Of course it's about cows," snorted Madge. "What about them?"

Bea unfolded a crumpled piece of paper. "If you'll kindly step back, I'll tell you."

Madge took a deep breath and stepped back.

"Mee, mee, mee," Bea warbled. "Mee, mee, mee. My poem is called *Getting Milked* and was written by me, me, me, Bea Holstein."

Getting milked
I find quite pleasin'.
I think it's the way
They does the squeezin'.

Bea bowed and the audience applauded.

"Now may I continue?" asked Madge. She stood closer to the microphone and handed Bea a piece of paper.

"This is a poem written and read by myself, Madge Holstein, and held up for me to read by my sister, Bea, who was born ten minutes after me."

Madge waited.

"What?"

"You're holding it upside down!"

"Oh, sorry," said Bea, turning the paper.

The crowd laughed and one of the hyenas made a rude comment about curdled milk. When everyone settled down, Madge began.

Nature's Baker
Manure in the meadow...

"Who?" interrupted Bea.

Madge stopped. She glared at Bea. "It's MY turn!"

"I was just wondering."

"Wondering what?"

"You said 'Ma knew her.'"

"I said... 'manure!'" Madge hissed.

"Ma knew who?"

"Who?"

"Who did Ma know?"

"How would I know?" shouted Madge.

The audience grew restless. They began whispering to each other. Big Vinnie moved slowly through the crowd.

"Well..." said Bea. "If Ma knew her, she must have been a friend. Although, I wonder if Ma only knew her in the meadow. I mean, maybe Ma knew her in town or on the farm or in a foreign country, like Kansas, or maybe..."

"BEA!"

"Wow!" said Moo. "What a performance…
a poem, a play, a sizzling dialog…"

"A family feud," added Minnie.

Madge glared at her sister. "Don't say another word!"

Bea held up the paper. Madge started again.

Nature's Baker
Manure in the meadow,
Sitting rich and steamy.
Meadow muffins baked
By nature's baker,
The wondrous cow.
A baker's dozen lie about,
Baking in the sun,
And when they're done,
They're free of charge,
So please,
have one.

76

The audience applauded cautiously, wondering if this was really the end of the Holsteins' performance.

"Now do you know what I'm talking about when I say manure?" asked Madge, as they walked off the stage.

"Of course," said Bea. "Manure, one of those little islands in Hawaii."

8

The "B" Word

Minnie and Moo both sat for a moment staring at the empty stage. "Wow," said Moo.

"That wasn't quite what I expected," admitted Minnie. "Still, it was very good and it was about cows." She marked her ballot.

When Moo tried to see how many points Minnie gave Bea and Madge, Minnie covered her paper. "No copying!"

"I wasn't copying," said Moo. "I was just curious."

Moo noticed two hyenas walking past the stage. When they saw Moo watching them, they elbowed each other and sniggered. They walked over to the far end of the stage and sat under the oak tree, whispering back and forth.

Minnie noticed them, too, and glanced over at the far side of the audience where most of the coyotes and weasels were sitting. Slick, the red fox, was waving his arms around as he talked to two weasels. One of them was carrying a tool kit.

"Up to no good," scowled Minnie.

"Where's the money box?"

"Same place it's been for the last half an hour. It's under my protection!"

"Who's next?" Moo changed the subject, looking at the schedule. She got up and walked over to the microphone. "Ah, Dog!" she announced and tucked the schedule into her toga.

"Dog?" some sheep yelled. "What about us? Why are we always the last to be called?"

"Because it takes a dog to make up your minds!" someone yelled.

"Meat eater!" cried a sheep.

"I love you, lamb chop!" shouted a coyote.

"Hear, hear," yelled Moo. "Let's be civil. This is for a good cause. Dog is next on the schedule. The sheep will follow."

"It's what they do best!" jeered a hyena.

Moo glanced over at the judges' table.

Minnie shrugged.

Moo took a deep breath. "And now," she announced, "it gives me great pleasure to introduce Dog, reciting an original poem."

Dog thanked Moo, Minnie, his friends, and the farmer. He gave a special thanks to his mother and waved. She smiled proudly.

"Boooo," called the three sheep that were waiting to go on next. "Bad dog!"

Moo raised her arms and they quieted down.

"Thank you," said Dog and gave a polite bow toward the sheep.

"Baaaaaaaaaad dog!" baaed the sheep.

If Dog heard them, he didn't react. He simply bowed again and said: "My poem is called *Captain Canine*. Thank you."

Who is the farmer's loyal friend?
Dog.
Who is faithful to the end?
Dog.
Yes, I'm the one,
the farmer's chum,
his closest aide,
unafraid
and proud,
PROUD,
to be called
Dog.
Who always knows
just what to do?
Who tends the sheep
while others sleep?
Dog.

Who herds the cows
with proud bow-wows?
Who guards the chicks
from foxy tricks?
Dog!
Yes, I am proud,
PROUD,
to be called Dog.
And every night,
when the job is done,
I croon the night
AWOOOOO.
The girls all swoon,
beneath the moon,
AWOOOOO, AWOOOOO,
AWOOOOOOOOOOOO.

Dog blew a kiss to his mother.

"Booooooooooo," bleated the sheep. "Double booooooooooooooo!"

The front rows of the audience burst into applause. The coyotes cheered, the hyenas hooted, and two weasels slipped into the shadows and crawled underneath the stage with a tool kit. They stopped under the judges' table where Minnie was sitting on the money box and took out a drill.

9

The Sheep's Protest Poem

Moo shook Dog's paw and thanked him for his song and for being so patient under such stressful circumstances.

"My pleasure," said Dog. He waved to his mother again and left the stage.

As he passed the sheep, one of them called him a rude name.

Moo muttered something about bad manners and then waved the sheep over to the center of the stage.

"About time," said one of the sheep. "This is our protest poem."

Why The Sheep Do Not Like Dog!
What do you expect,
You silly mutt,
When you bite us
On the ...

"WHOA! WHOA!" shouted Minnie. "We'll have none of THAT kind of language!"

A look of confusion crossed the sheep's fuzzy faces.

Minnie stood up and pointed to a spot in front of her. "Come over here!"

The sheep walked slowly to the judges' stand, looking sheepish and confused. They mumbled to each other, but didn't say anything to Minnie.

"I'll have none of that in THIS festival," Minnie said. She leaned closer to Moo and whispered, "They were going to use the 'b' word."

"The 'b' word?"

Minnie nodded knowingly. She whispered the "b" word into Moo's ear.

"It's just a word," said Moo. "It rhymes with 'mutt.'"

A crowd began to gather near the stage. They strained to hear what the judges were saying.

"I don't care," insisted Minnie. "There are

children here... kids, calves, chicks, piglets, bunnies, puppies, and, and...polliwogs."

"Polliwogs?"

"Moo, this is a family festival. If they are going to refer to that part of a person's anatomy, they should use the proper term...gluteus maximus."

"What's a gluteus maximus?" one of the sheep asked. "A Roman gladiator?"

A hyena stood up and shouted. "The muscles in your..."

"THAT'S ENOUGH!" interrupted Minnie.

Little Vinnie moved toward the hyenas.

Moo leaned back in her chair. "Minnie, poetry needs to be free and expressive. I don't think we should tell others what to write or what not to write. Besides, gluteus maximus doesn't rhyme with 'mutt.'"

"Coconut does…they could use the word 'coconut.' It's symbolic. Coconuts are hairy. Sheep are woolly. Get it? It makes perfect sense."

Minnie walked over to the microphone and repeated the poem.

What do you expect,
You silly mutt,
When you bite us
On the coconut?

Bea and Madge Holstein and several cows from the Wilkerson's farm applauded lightly.

Everyone else stared at each other. When Minnie sat down and nodded proudly at Bea and Madge, Bea and Madge waved back.

"No offense," said Moo, "but it sounds flat."

"No buts about it!" commented Dog.

The hyenas laughed so hard, they fell off their chairs. They stopped laughing when they saw Big Vinnie heading toward them.

"Look," said one of the sheep, "he didn't bite us on the coconut, he bit us on the…"

Minnie glared at the sheep.

"…Roman gladiator," finished another sheep.

"That's not true," yelled Dog. "It was a nip, a little nip on their Roman gladiator."

"Yeah," shouted a hyena. "A little nip on the gladiator never hurt anyone."

"Yeah!" a coyote shouted. "What did you expect, you silly sheep? Who do you think he is, Little Bo-Peep?"

All the weasels began to giggle again.

"Oh, butt out," said the biggest sheep.

"THAT'S IT!" shouted Minnie.

Moo sighed.

"Minnie, please, it's their poem. Try to be more open-minded. Just because we all grew up on different farms doesn't mean we can't all get along.

One person's bark is another's baaa. See? Please. Try. If you don't like it, you can give them a low score."

Minnie scooped up her pencil and sat down. She muttered something about bad taste. When she tried writing a zero on her paper, the pencil broke.

Moo waved her arm toward the sheep.

"Please," she said, "try it again. It's your poem."

She started to walk away, but returned to the microphone. "And please, no more comments. Try to be polite."

Everyone went back to their places. The sheep adjusted the microphone. They all cleared their throats at the same time and tried again.

Why The Sheep

Do Not Like Dog!

What do you expect,

You silly mutt,

When you bite us

On the

"NEXT!" Minnie shouted.

10

King Of The Road

Moo stared at Minnie.

"Will you relax?"

"It's not proper," Minnie mumbled. She picked up another pencil and marked her scorecard.

"What's not proper?"

"Certain words read in public."

"They're just words," said Moo.

"Not in my book!"

"Minnie, be honest, when was the last time you read a book?"

"That has nothing to do with it! If I had a book, I'd cross the words out!"

"Why?"

"To protect the children!"

"From what?" Moo asked.

"From reading them, of course!"

"Minnie, what do you think would happen if they did read them?"

"Something!"

"Like?"

"Crime!" exclaimed Minnie. "I hate the idea of so many children's lives ruined by reading!"

Moo sighed.

"Books are stuffed with words, Moo!"

"Minnie, what's the matter? What are you worried about now? And don't tell me it's about children reading, because we both know that's not true!"

"Oh," Minnie moaned. "You're right, I am worried. And to tell you the truth, sitting on this money box isn't very comfortable, either."

Minnie stood up and rubbed her gluteus maximus. She looked back at the two hyenas that were still watching them from the foot of the oak tree. "They make me nervous. They're up to something!"

"Who?"

"Those hyenas," said Minnie, sitting back down. "And where did those other weasels go that were carrying that tool box? I don't like it, Moo!"

"Relax, the Boarzinni brothers are out there. Have another cream puff."

"You're right. Maybe that's it. I should eat something to keep me calm. I could use the protein." Minnie reached into the bag and took out two cream puffs. "Who's next?"

Moo stared at her friend for a moment, shook her head, and then picked up the schedule. "Porkus Hockus. He sings and plays the blues." She waved to Porkus who was sitting with the band.

"What's that sawing noise I hear?" Minnie mumbled, looking under her chair. "I see sawdust. I think we have termites."

"They're probably after your éclairs," Moo said absently. She waved at Porkus again.

Porkus picked up his guitar and stepped off the bandstand. He strolled over to the judges' table and tipped his fedora. "Miss Minnie," he said smoothly. "Miss Moo. How y'all doin' today?"

"Fine, thank you," said Minnie. "And you?"

"Me?" Porkus seemed startled by the question. "Me? Most blue. I is the 'i' in music."

"Most blue!" Moo nodded. "The blues man."

"Yeah," said Porkus, sauntering back across the stage. He sat down on a stool. "The blues man." He sighed, playing a few melancholy chords on his guitar and smiling.

The music seemed to have a life of its own, smoothly sailing from one bit of song to another. It was as though Porkus were searching, waiting as the music floated by, alert, ready to snag a certain sad memory as it drifted along.

"You know," he said gently, "sometimes we all get down. We all get the blues. Sometimes the blues seem to last forever. But other times the blues is about something that brought you joy.

"Something you remember, but don't have anymore, like your first car. My first car was an Oldsmobile Rocket 88. Oh man, how I loved that car. Red vinyl seats and 300 horsepower, bumper to bumper, chrome to chrome.

"So here it is, *King of the Road*, and if you feel heat in your feets, it means they longs to dance, so get up, give in, and let your feet do the talking."

Porkus sang:

I'm drivin' a rocket with red vinyl seats,
And 300 horses are rockin' the beat.
Rockin' and rollin' down the interstate,
Laughin' and drivin' my Olds 88.
'Cause everything's cool, everything's great,
I'm king of the road in my Olds 88.

It's lollipop red, channeled and chopped,
And bumper to bumper, rakishly dropped.
Purple blue flames, man, they look good,
Spread out across the supercharged hood.
'Cause everything's cool, everything's great,
I'm king of the road in my Olds 88.

My girlfriend's name is on the front door,
Pin-striped pink, she knows the score.
If she ever leaves me and ain't no more,
I'll just find another named Eleanor.
'Cause everything's cool, everything's great,
I'm king of the road in my Olds 88.

Bumper to bumper, chrome to chrome,
This car and me was made to roam.
And when I die and can't roam no more,
I'll rocket to heaven in my red meteor.
'Cause everything's cool, everything's great,
I'm king of the road in my Olds 88.

When all God's children see my Olds 88,
They'll shout to the Lord, "Open the gate!"
All the angels in heaven will be singing this song.
We'll be rockin' together, all night long.
'Cause everything's cool, everything's great,
I'm king of the road in my Olds 88.
Bumper to bumper, chrome to chrome,
I'm king of the road in my Olds 88.
Bumper to bumper, chrome to chrome,
I'm king of the road in my Olds 88.

The crowd went wild. The coyotes and the hyenas kept shouting for more. One of the coyotes was smoking a cigar and when he offered it to a group of puppies, Big Vinnie made him put it out. There was a tussle and Big Vinnie sent the coyote sailing over the first two rows.

Minnie tugged on Moo's toga. "Moo! Did you see that?"

Moo put her pencil down. "No. What did you see?"

"The same thing I always see," complained Minnie. "Trouble!"

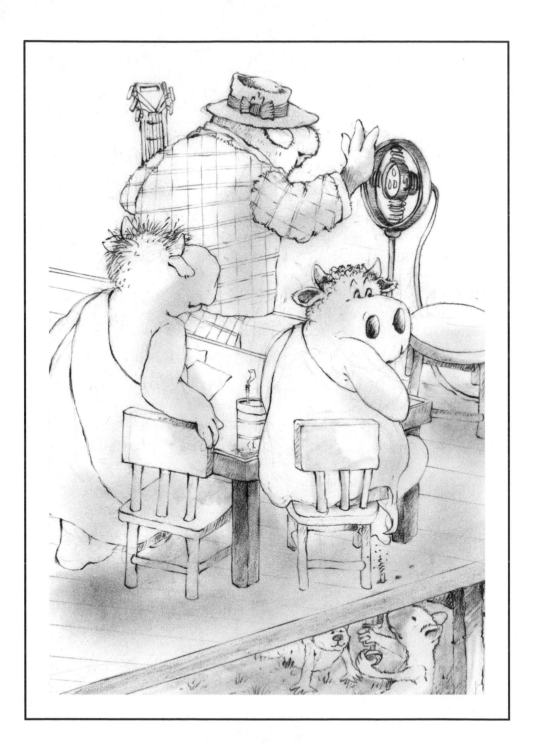

11

Termites

Porkus smiled and began playing softly on his harmonica. The doleful, laconic notes drifted down onto the audience like a sweet summer rain. The crowd grew silent.

"The blues is about moving on, too..." said Porkus, "about being a 'rolling stone,' about lost love, love found, and love lost again."

He played a few chords on his guitar and then looked out into the audience. "You know what I mean, baby..."

"I do!" called a voice from the crowd.

Minnie strained to see who it was. "Darn," she whispered. "I wonder who he was talking to? Do you think it was his girlfriend? Do you think it's one of the Holsteins? Bea has been kind of moody lately."

"Minnie, please."

"What? I was just wondering." Minnie wiggled in her chair. "What's the matter with this thing? The legs seem loose. And what's that sawing noise I keep hearing?"

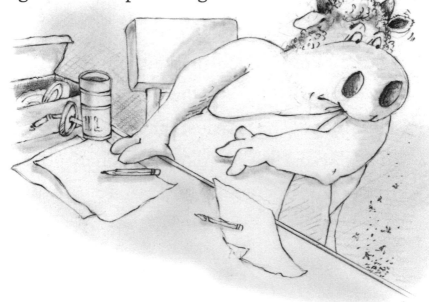

Moo stood up. "Listen to the crowd, they love Porkus. Sing another one," Moo shouted.

Porkus smiled and nodded toward Moo. He hummed as he played, not singing anything in particular, letting the notes lead him wherever they wanted to go.

"What is that noise?" Minnie muttered. "What's going on here?"

Under the stage, one of the weasels finished sawing a hole underneath Minnie's chair. Another reached through the hole and grabbed the leg of the chair.

"Higher," whispered the first weasel.

The second weasel reached up and stretched as high as he could.

"Minnie," said Moo. "Hand me my notes."

Minnie stood up, reached across the table, and picked up the list.

The weasel squeezed his head through the hole and then his arm. "I see the box."

"Hurry up," whispered the other. "Grab it!"

Minnie sat down and the chair collapsed in a puff of sawdust. She tumbled to the floor. There was a muffled scream from under the broken chair.

Moo ran over and picked up the money box and set it on the table. Then she pulled Minnie up and set her down on another chair. "Are you all right? What happened?"

"I don't know. It must have been those cream puffs."

Porkus stopped playing. "Miss Minnie, are you okay?"

"I'm fine," Minnie grumbled. "Anybody want to split this éclair? I'm cutting back."

Moo pointed at the First Aid Booth. "Now what? Look, they're carrying two weasels into the tent."

"Trouble," growled Minnie. She pulled the money box a little closer. "You've got to watch those weasels like a hawk!"

12

Minnie Sings

The air grew cooler as the sun set behind the western hills. The crowd moved closer to the stage to hear Porkus's next song. Nadine, the water buffalo, and some of the larger animals had moved the tables and set them up in a semicircle at the foot of the hill by the booths. The last of the food and drinks were piled on the tables. Nadine made a sign that said: *Help Yourself… Free!*

"It's starting to get dark," said Minnie. "How many more before we wrap this up?"

"A few," said Moo, reading the schedule.

"And then?"

"Then we light the Tiki torches while the moon comes up, and Irene and the band will play dance music, and then we announce the winners."

Minnie looked into the crowd. "They're pretty quiet out there. We need to pep them up."

"Porkus can do that."

"I know just the song!"

Moo nodded toward Porkus who returned the nod. He began playing again, tinkering with a melody and talking to the crowd as though they were all sitting around, chatting about old times.

"*The Jungle Jives!*" Minnie announced.

Porkus looked up and smiled.

"Only if you sing it with me!"

"Oh!" gulped Minnie. "I'm not much of a..."

"Go on," Moo urged.

"Ladies and gents," said Porkus, still strumming on his guitar. "This here song is called *The Jungle Jives*. But I can't sing it alone. It's a duet. I was thinkin' maybe you might encourage Miss Minnie to help me out."

The audience came alive at the prospect and cheered for Minnie to sit down with Porkus and sing. They applauded and didn't stop until Minnie stood up and walked across the stage.

"Oh my," she said. "I think this is a mistake."

Moo stood up and clapped.

Minnie sat on a stool next to Porkus. He glanced back at Irene and winked. Irene nodded and pointed at Moe, the gorilla, who began playing the tom toms as an introduction to the music.

"Miss Minnie and I are going to sing, but you out there ain't gettin' off the hook, neither. Help us out! All together now! Ready?"

"Ready!" the audience shouted.

"How 'bout you, Miss Minnie?"

Minnie gulped.

Moe, the drummer, kept up his steady beat.

"Yeah," said Porkus. "It's gettin' kinda warm up here. Must be that jungle beat."

Must be feelin' that jungle heat,
Must be feelin' that jungle beat,
Musta caught them jungle jives,
Look a' them feets, they's alive!
Look a' that snake, spinnin' spinnin'.
Look a' that hyena, grinnin' grinnin'.
Look a' that tiger, prowlin' prowlin'.
Look a' that wolf, howlin' howlin'.
Look a' them frogs, leapin' leapin'.
Look a' them lizards, creepin' creepin'.

They must be feelin' that jungle heat,
They must be feelin' that jungle beat,
They musta caught them jungle jives,
Look a' them feets, they's alive!

Look a' that hippo, hoppin' hoppin',
Look a' that rhino, boppin' boppin'.
Look a' that dog, howlin' howlin',
Look a' that cat, meowin' meowin'.
Look a' that monkey, swingin' swingin',
Look at us now! We're singin' singin'!

We must be feelin' the jungle heat.
We musta caught the jungle beat.
We musta caught them jungle jives.
Look a' them feets, they's alive!

It's the ZOOM ZOOM of that jungle heat.
It's the BOOM BOOM of that jungle beat.
Look a' them feets, they's alive!

BOOM BOOM

The audience jumped up and cheered.

Porkus thanked Minnie as she took a brief bow. She plopped down next to Moo.

Moo threw her arms around Minnie. "That was incredible! You were wonderful. I didn't know you could sing."

"I do have a few secrets," Minnie wheezed.

13

One-Eyed Charlie

Porkus glanced back at the judges' table.

"One more, please," Moo pleaded.

Porkus nodded, turned back to the audience, and began playing little strings of notes on his guitar.

"You all heard the rumors about that bad, bad man they calls One-Eyed Charlie," he said. "You have, haven't you? Yes, One-Eyed Charlie, the butcher. He ain't no friend to any of us. He sure ain't no friend to the Porcine family. Unn uhhh!"

The crowd murmured to each other in hushed, serious tones.

Some of the sheep began to whisper about a strange rumor that had circulated last year concerning the farmer's new wool coat.

Bea wondered aloud to Madge about the disappearance of their older brother Mel from the Flat-Landers Farm.

All the little pigs in the audience sat closer to the big pigs.

Even the coyotes grew quiet. One of them told a brief story to a big buck sitting next to him about three of his brothers who disappeared in Montana.

"Hey," said the buck. "You ever heard of deer season?"

Porkus didn't seem to mind all the mutterings in the crowd. Soon it was quiet.

"No," he said. "One-eyed Charlie ain't no friend to any of us. This here song was sung to me by my Uncle Rufus P. Porcine when I was a boy south of Wilkerson's farm...*Movin' On*."

Time to say so long,
Time to say good-bye.
Time to sing this sad, sad song,
Time to end the lullaby.
I see my future, sweetheart,
It don't look good to me.
It's time to go, time to part,
Good-bye, my honey bee.
Don't take no crystal ball,
Don't take no PhD,
No handwriting on the wall,
To see what I can see.

You see them pork rinds?
Them deep fried chitlins?
Take a look at them chili dogs,
Sittin' in Charlie's window.
See them chops? See them hocks?
You hear that sizzlin', baby?
That's my bacon fryin' in that pan.
You smell that barbecue, sweetheart?
That red-eye gravy, nice and thick?
Guess who, sweetstuff?
I'm that corn dog,
Sittin' on that stick.
It's why I'm packed,
It's why I'm leavin'.
I see my future, baby,
And it don't look good to me.
Unnn uhhh,
It just don't look good to me.

"More!" shouted the audience. "We've been there, man, sing to us..."

Porkus stood up and waved. "That one was for you, baby," he declared. "And you, and you, and you!" He walked back to the bandstand, humming to himself.

Moo sniffed. "Life is so like that!"

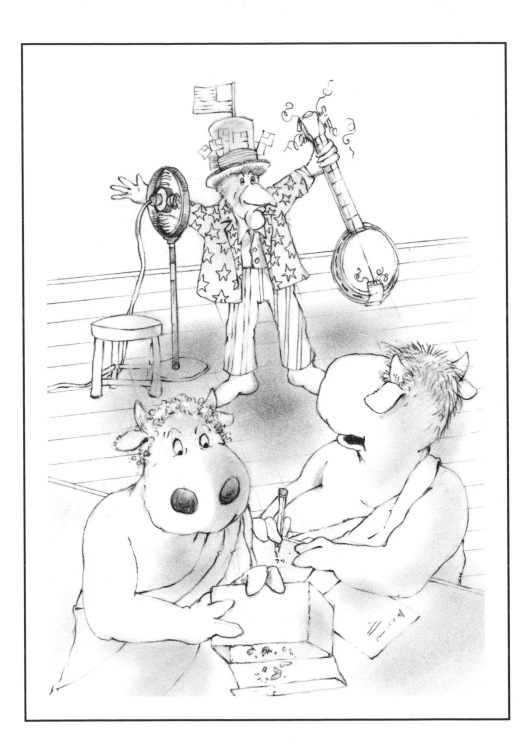

14

Uncle Spam

Minnie picked up the bakery box. She turned the box upside down and crumbs fell out. "Moo, did you eat both those Danishes?"

"No, I…"

"Thank you, thank you," crowed a voice over the loudspeaker.

"It's Elvis!" moaned Moo. "It's not his turn."

"Moo, are you sure you didn't eat both those Danishes? One had apricot filling and one had raspberry. I remember them distinctly."

Minnie crawled under the table. "Maybe they fell down here. Help me find them, Moo. Can't you see I'm starving?"

Elvis pointed at three of the Poulettes. They were dressed in red cowgirl boots, red vinyl mini skirts, and fluffy blue blouses with white stars. He began strumming on a banjo with only one string.

"Thanks so much, Porky Forkus, for that terrific rendition of *Blue America*. Speaking of America, let's hear it for good old Uncle Spam.

"That's me, Elvis Rooster, pretending to be Uncle Spam, doing an original country western song, written by me and played by me on this here American banjo, you all."

He plucked away while he chatted, imitating Porkus. "This here is called *God Bless America*, 'cause I met a chick named Sue, wearing an orange flour sack, by the side of the road, picking up trash for the Department of Corrections and was immediately attracted to her because of her cooking, even though she was really, really ugly."

Moo looked under the table while Elvis sang.

I got me a sweetheart
Who's red, white, and blue,
An American chicken,
A flag-waving Sue.
She's not much to look at,
That's certainly true,
But man, can she cook.
Try her pelican stew!

She lost a leg
In eighty-eight,
Is bald as a cucumber
And overweight.
She has a pin in her hip
And only one eye,
But what do I care?
You should taste that pie!

I got me a sweetheart
Who's red, white, and blue,
An American chicken,
A flag-waving Sue.

God bless Uncle Spam,
And God bless Sue,
God bless America,
And the barbecue.

She's an American chicken,
A flag-waving booster.
I thank heaven above,
I'm an American rooster.

God bless Uncle Spam,
And God bless Sue,
God bless America,
And God bless you.

There was light applause from the geese and the ducks in the third row and from the rest of the chickens who, for some reason, had forgiven Elvis for his comments about Meg.

"Ha!" hooted Minnie, from under the table. "I found one! It's still good! No one stepped on it!" She pulled herself up and sat down in another chair. "What's Elvis doing out there?"

"He just sang another song," complained Moo. "You missed it while you were on your search for the lost Danish."

Minnie turned over the Danish and brushed off some bits of dried leaves. "Where's the money box?"

"Minnie! You had it! You were sitting on it!"

"A ut et ot ta maple," Minnie mumbled.

"What?"

Minnie swallowed. "I left it on the table."

"It's gone!"

"What?"

Minnie looked under the table while Moo searched under the papers on the judges' table.

"Oh no," Minnie moaned.

"And one more for the road," Elvis cooed, still standing in the middle of the stage.

"Doesn't he ever go away?" asked Moo.

Elvis plucked the banjo while the Poulettes hummed and swayed in the background.

"This is an old American folk song called *I Had a One-Legged Dog named Hoppy That Hated Brussels Sprouts, But Didn't Mind Okra if...*"

"Hey!" Minnie shouted. "It's not your turn!"

Elvis stopped strumming. "What?"

"It's not your turn," repeated Moo, lifting her chair, looking for the money box.

"There's nobody else up here!"

"We are," piped up two hyenas waiting at the edge of the stage.

"I believe it's our turn," said Slick, the red fox. He held up the schedule sheet and pointed at his name. "We're next."

"Ah, we're a little busy right now," Minnie snapped.

Slick walked across the stage and stopped at the judges' table. "Look under Miss Minnie's collapsed chair," he advised and smiled.

Minnie pushed the seat of the broken chair aside and found the money box. "Talk about luck," she said, holding up the box. "The apricot Danish is stuck to the top and it's still good!"

15

Elvis Gets Sawed In Half

Slick winked at Minnie. "Lucky you."

"I guess," said Minnie, picking off a twig from the Danish.

Moo checked the schedule. "Let's see. Aha! A magic act. Is that right?"

Slick nodded.

"And jokes," added a hyena.

Moo waved to Irene and the band played an introductory tune.

"Hey!" called Elvis. "What about me?"

"Stick around," said Slick. "You can be part of the magic show. We'll make you a star!"

"Really? What do I have to do?"

"Take off your pants!"

"My pants?"

"And your shoes," said the fox. "You and the girls wait over there."

"That's it? All I have to do to become a star is take off my pants and my shoes?"

"All eyes will be on you!"

Elvis sighed. "A star at last."

"I don't like this," Minnie fretted. She pulled the money box a little closer and tried to wipe off a wad of apricot stuck to the lid.

"And now, ladies and gentlemen," announced Slick, "I'd like to introduce you to Hee and Haw for a few laughs while we get ready to perform our most amazing feats of magic."

The coyotes pushed a big box onto the stage behind Hee and Haw. Slick nodded to the hyenas and they stepped up to the microphone.

"So," said Hee. "Tell me, Haw, what's the most important use of cowhide?"

"Don't know, Hee. What?"

"To hold the cow together!" The two hyenas roared with laughter.

"What's so funny about that?" Minnie asked.

Moo shrugged. "I don't know."

Except for the cows, the audience laughed, too.

"Hey, Hee, did you hear about the cow that said 'baa?'"

"No. Why would a cow say 'baa?'"

"She said 'baa' because she was learning a foreign language! Get it? A foreign language!"

"I don't think that's funny," said a sheep.

"Me, either," said a cow.

"Hey! What does a duck do when he flies upside down?" Hee asked.

"I don't know. Tell me," said Haw.

"He quacks up!"

"Now that's funny," said one of the sheep.

"No, it isn't," quacked a duck.

"Where's your sense of humor?" asked a cow.

140

Hee held up his hand and shook his head. "I got a question, Haw. Maybe you can help me answer it."

"I'll try. Go ahead. What's the question?"

"What kind of fur do we get from skunks?"

"That's a tough one. I don't know, Hee. What kind of fur do we get from skunks?"

"As 'fur' away as we can get!" shouted Hee. The two hyenas laughed so hard, they had to hold each other up.

"Now that was funny!" honked a goose.

"I didn't think so," snapped a skunk.

Slick walked up to the microphone. "Thanks, Hee and Haw. You were terrific. Absolutely terrific. How about it, folks? Weren't they great?"

The crowd applauded their approval.

"And now for a little magic," Slick announced. The two coyotes pushed the wooden box toward the front of the stage. The Poulettes danced and giggled as they pointed to the box and blew kisses to the audience.

"For our first astounding piece of magic, I'll need a volunteer, someone with talent, handsome, young, energetic, brilliant, and..."

"That's me!" Elvis shouted.

"Are you sure?" the fox asked.

"Of course," said Elvis. "I already took off my shoes and pants. What's next?"

"Just climb into this wooden box. Stick your head out of this end and your legs out the two holes at the other end."

"That's it?"

"That's it!" said Slick.

"Piece of cake," snickered Elvis.

Slick nodded toward the band. They played the theme from the Twilight Zone. Elvis climbed into the box, and the coyotes closed and locked the lid. Elvis's head hung out of one end and a pair of fake chicken feet hung out the other.

"This is easy. Am I a star yet?"

"Not quite," said Slick.

"Well, hurry up! I don't have all day."

"Ready?"

"Of course! Let's get this show on the road."

Slick picked up a long saw, wiggling it back and forth so it made an eerie sound.

"Whoa, whoa!" yelped Elvis. "What's that for?"

"This? This extra long, extra sharp saw?"

"Yes! That one. Are you going to cut down a tree or something?"

"I'm going to cut something in half."

"Like?"

"Like this box."

Elvis nodded. "Oh, I see."

The fox put the saw blade on the edge of the box. "I'm glad."

"Wait a second. I'm in the box."

"Yes, you are."

"But if you cut the box in half, I'll be…"

Slick smiled. "Yes, you will."

144

"Aggggg!" Elvis screamed. "Let me out!"

"I thought you wanted to be a star. I thought you wanted to be rich and famous."

"What good is it to be rich if I'm in two pieces?!"

"If you're in two pieces," declared the fox, "you'll be twice as rich!"

"Really?"

"Of course. Isn't two twice as much as one?"

"You're right!"

"Ready?"

"Will it hurt?"

"Only at first. After that, you won't feel a thing."

The fox drew the blade across the wooden box, marking the place he intended to cut.

Elvis screamed.

"I haven't started yet," said Slick.

"Oh."

Slick sawed. The saw squeaked and swooshed. Sawdust fell to the floor with each stroke of the saw. Elvis screamed louder.

He was still screaming after Slick sawed the box in half and the two halves were pulled apart. Elvis's head hung out of the first box and the pair of fake chicken feet still hung out of the other, with nothing but air between the two boxes.

"You can stop screaming now," said Slick. "We're done."

"That wasn't so bad," boasted Elvis. "I hardly felt a thing!"

16

The Magic Boxes

The coyotes pushed the boxes back together and shoved them toward the rear of the stage. They picked up two smaller boxes and set them in front. One box was covered with a red silk cloth and the other with a black one.

As the sky darkened, they lit Tiki torches.

The fox put on his wizard's hat and cloak. He smiled at Minnie and Moo.

"Did you enjoy that?" asked the fox.

"Wonderful," said Moo.

"I still don't trust him," Minnie whispered. She smiled back at the fox.

"Here we have two boxes," Slick announced. "A black box and a red box, both the same size and both empty." One of the Poulettes pulled off the red cloth and opened the box, tilting it so the audience could see it was empty. Then she replaced the cloth.

Slick moved to the second box. Another Poulette pulled the black cloth away with a flourish, while a different Poulette opened the lid to the box and again tilted it to show the audience that it, too, was empty.

Slick nodded thoughtfully. "Simple enough. But where's the magic? Ah, yes, the magic. Well, I'll tell you. I intend to put something in the red box, lock it, and without touching either box, move the object from the red box to the black box!"

"Right," Minnie muttered.

The fox put his paw on the red box. "Now let's see. What can we put in this box? Something valuable? Something like a watch or a…"

"Money box," shouted one of the coyotes.

The fox looked over at Minnie and Moo and smiled. "How about it, girls? Trust me?"

Moo shrugged. "Sure."

"No," said Minnie.

"You can put it in yourself," Slick offered. "And you can stand right next to me. After I say the magic words, you can open the second box, take your money box, and return it to the table."

"Go ahead," said Moo. "What can happen? You're standing right there."

"Okay." Minnie waved to the side of the stage where Big Vinnie and Little Vinnie were waiting. "I want them next to the coyotes. I'll not stand for any hanky panky."

The fox made a sad face. "I'm sorry you don't trust me after all I've done for this charity. I have to be honest, Miss Minnie. The world would be a better place if you trusted others a little more."

Minnie waved the Boarzinni brothers closer. She carried the money box to the center of the stage, pulled off the red cloth, and opened the red box.

"Go ahead," said Slick. "Trust me."

Everyone gathered around the red box and watched Minnie put in the money box. She closed the lid, locked it, and put back the red cloth.

"Little Vinnie," she warned. "Don't take your eyes off this box."

Slick waved to the band and they struck up another eerie tune. "Stand back a little," he directed. "Give the magic room to work."

The audience was silent. Strange music played in the background while Slick closed his eyes and began to utter strange, powerful magic words. He spread his red-robed arms. "Hocus Pocus, Domin Occus, Judies Mucus, oh, invisible spirit, move the most precious money box from the magic red box to the magic black box."

"NOW!" Slick shouted. Six Tiki torches burst into flame. There was a puff of smoke from both boxes. The red cloth and the black cloth flew up and then gently drifted to the floor.

"Open the black box!"

"I'll open it!" said Minnie, "And the money box better be in there!" She glanced over at the Boarzinni brothers. "Or else!"

Minnie unlocked the black box.

"OH!" she gasped, lifting out the money box. She held it high in the air for the audience to see.

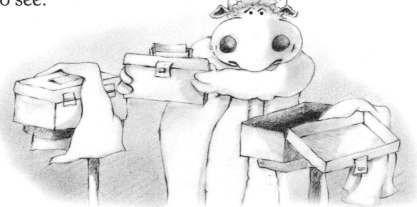

The crowd was astonished.

"Wow!" Moo applauded. "That was terrif-ic!"

The fox grinned. "Thank you. Our pleasure. When we help others, we help ourselves."

The Poulettes left the stage, tiptoeing past Elvis who was fast asleep, his head hanging down from one end of the box.

Moo took the money box and sat back down at the judges' table. The coyotes removed the magic equipment, took one last bow, and shoved the snoring Elvis against the backstage curtains.

Slick winked at Minnie and walked away.

"See," said Moo. "You should learn to trust others more. Try giving people a second chance. You heard what the fox said. When we help others, we help ourselves. That's important to remember, Minnie. I'm going to give them a 10."

"Maybe you're right," Minnie admitted, picking up the money box. "They even cleaned it."

"Cleaned it?"

"Cleaned it," repeated Minnie. "There was apricot jam on the lid and now it's gone."

Moo picked up the money box and looked at it carefully. "Cleaned it? But when and why?"

Minnie picked up her scorecard. "Just try-ing to be nice, I guess. All part of that thing about helping yourself when you help others."

"I have a bad feeling about this," said Moo.

"What do you mean?"

"Where's the key to the lock?"

"On a little chain in my pocket. Why?"

Moo took a deep breath. "I hope I'm wrong."

Minnie pulled the chain out of her pocket and handed it to Moo. Moo tried to insert the key into the lock, but it wouldn't fit. She tried again and again, but it was no use.

"Oh my," she sighed. "This is a different box! We've been robbed!"

17

The Chase

Minnie and Moo stared at the fake box.

"Robbed?" said Minnie. "But…"

"They switched money boxes," explained Moo, handing back the key chain. She fell back into her chair and moaned. "It's all my fault. And now they're long gone!"

Minnie jumped up from the table. "Not yet, they aren't! Listen." The sound of hyenas laughing was drowned out by the roar of motorcycles revving up at the edge of the audience.

A motorcycle roared up the hill and spun around and around, throwing dirt into the air and onto the stage. Slick held up the money box.

"So long, you big schnooks!" he yelled and roared away. Two black-leathered coyotes waved as they whooshed by on their motorcycles. Right behind them raced the two hyenas named Hee and Haw on a motorcycle with a sidecar. They slowed down in front of the stage, pointed at Minnie and laughed.

"So long, fatso!" yelled Hee.

"AGGGGGG!" Minnie screamed and leaped off the stage. She fell on top of the two hyenas, and the motorcycle sputtered to a stop. She pulled them out and put them both in a headlock, squeezing hard.

"Help, help," the hyenas gasped.

Little Vinnie and his brother ran up and tried pulling the two hyenas away from Minnie, but she refused to let go. She tossed them over her head, sat on them, and then bounced up and down.

"Nobody calls me fat and gets away with it!"

161

Moo ran up and helped the Boarzinni brothers drag the hyenas out from under Minnie.

"Quick!" Minnie shouted. "Get in!"

Moo climbed into the sidecar and Minnie jumped onto the motorcycle.

"Go, go, go!" Moo yelled.

The motorcycle roared away.

Minnie leaned forward and the motorcycle shot ahead, 50, 60, 65.

"Faster!"

The motorcycle screamed closer and closer to the coyotes, 70, 75, 80, 85!

"Are you crazy?" cried one of the coyotes. The two coyotes tried to turn away. They veered off and crashed through a rail fence and tumbled into the muddy middle of a pigpen.

"Don't stop!" Moo shouted, "Faster! Faster!"

Minnie roared on. "Do you see the fox?"

"I can hear him! It's getting too dark to see. There! He's cutting through the apple orchard. Faster, Minnie, faster!"

Minnie went faster.

When the fox heard Minnie and Moo coming up behind him, he tore through the orchard.

But Minnie went faster. Just as she pulled up behind the fox, he sped up a hill and across a bumpy hay field. Dust billowed up. Minnie rode through it without slowing down.

"Cut him off at the barn!" Moo yelled.

Minnie plowed through a haystack and onto the road. The motorcycle skidded to a stop, throbbing and coughing as it idled. They waited in the shadows as Slick came tearing out of the field toward the barn.

"Here he comes!" warned Moo.

Minnie revved the motorcycle higher and higher, leaned forward, and just as Slick came speeding by, she accelerated so fast, the motorcycle popped a wheelie.

"Yeow!" shouted Slick as he threw the money box into the air.

Minnie pulled over. "Quick, check it out!"

Moo jumped out and grabbed the box. She tried to fit the key into the muddy lock.

"Hurry! He's getting away!"

Moo cleaned off the lock and the key slipped in. She turned the lock and it snapped open.

The box was empty.

18

The Crash

"It's a trick!" Moo shouted. "He's got the money!" She threw down the empty box and jumped into the sidecar. "Go, go, go!"

They roared down the road.

Slick turned to see if Minnie and Moo were still behind him. He could see their headlight bearing down on him. When he turned back, he saw a huge oak tree, and his motorcycle was headed straight toward it. He veered to the left and hit a rock.

The motorcycle sailed end over end, sending the fox flying through the air. He landed in the middle of the curtains, pulling them down and rolling into the center of the stage.

Elvis stood in front of him wearing half of the magic box. "Hey! You said I was going to be famous! So far all I got out of this was sawed in half and a set of wooden underwear. I think I got a splinter. I want my legs back!"

Slick shook his head. He could hear loud, angry voices. Where could he run, where could he hide? The Boarzinni brothers were rushing toward the stage and he could hear the sound of a motor-cycle getting closer and closer!

Slick pulled himself up and glanced around quickly. There, the other half of the big box trick, he could hide in there, easy.

Minnie and Moo roared to a stop behind the stage.

Slick ran over to the big box with the pair of fake chicken legs sticking out, climbed in, and slammed the lid closed so hard, the lock snapped shut and the fake chicken legs fell out.

Elvis moved over to the second box and looked at the pair of legs lying on the floor. He picked one up, turning it over and over.

"There's something fishy going on here," he

muttered. "These don't look like my legs. My legs are younger, longer, and they bend."

"Hey, Slick!" he shouted, pounding on the lid of the box with one of the chicken legs. "These aren't my legs. I know my legs when I see them!"

"Go away!" whispered the fox.

Elvis kept on pounding with the fake legs. "I want my legs back! Gimmie my legs back or I'll sue you for loss of personal property!"

"You're standing on them, you moron," hissed the fox. "Go away!"

Minnie and Moo climbed onto the stage. The Boarzinni brothers ran up and met them in the middle of the platform next to Elvis.

Elvis stepped out of the wooden box. "That feels so much better," he said, rubbing his legs. He knocked on the side of the box the fox was hiding in. "Thanks, I found them!"

Moo pointed at a fuzzy fox tail hanging out of one of the leg holes in the box.

Little Vinnie opened the box.

"Hi!" said Slick, innocently. "I was just hav-
ing a little fun. Here's your money!"

Big Vinnie dragged the fox away. A large
crowd had gathered at the foot of the stage as the
Poulettes rushed up and hugged Elvis.

"Our hero!" they clucked and smothered
him with kisses.

"What?" said Elvis.

"You saved the day," said a chicken.

"I did?"

"Yes, the fox took the money box."

"He did?"

"Stole it!"

"He tried to steal my legs, too," whined Elvis, "but I got them back! Nobody steals my legs and gets away with it!"

The band played *America the Beautiful.*

Elvis picked up the microphone and waved.

"Don't tell me he's going to give a speech," moaned Moo.

The music died down and Elvis blew a kiss to the audience. "You do love me," he said and then began to sing.

All of me, I found all of me.
I thought I lost my bottom,
I thought I lost my legs,
But now we're reunited.
I feel so excited.
From the bottom to the top...
We're together again.

All of me, oh how I love all of me.
All of me, oh...

"Thanks so much," said Minnie, grabbing the microphone.

"Wait," protested Elvis. "I have ten more verses. They're fresh, I just made them up, I'm on a roll, everybody loves me. Have you seen my bag-pipes?"

19

Aloha

Minnie handed Moo the microphone.

"Thanks so much for your patience," she said to the crowd. "Sorry about that little incident with the money box. Now while we add up the scores to see who are tonight's winners, Irene and the band will play dance music for you all. Nadine will light the bonfire. The food is free, so enjoy yourselves! Feel free to dance the light fandango, the chicken flap, the whatever. Give Irene your requests, the band can play it all."

"Aloha!" yelled Elvis as he danced back onto the stage wearing a grass skirt and twirling a flaming torch in each hand. "Tiki, tiki, hanuka-ha! The dance of the flaming chicken feet! Hooka hooka!" Elvis danced in front of the Poulettes. The drummer kept up a Polynesian drum beat as Elvis stomped about on the stage. He tossed one of the torches into the air. "Hot Chihuahua!" he yelled. "Hot Tiki Mama!"

"Doesn't he ever give up?" asked Moo.

"He makes me nervous," said Minnie.

A spark from one of the torches landed in Elvis's grass skirt. Smoke billowed up from behind him as he bounced around on the stage.

Moo grabbed the fire extinguisher, aimed it at the twirling Elvis, and pulled the trigger.

Just as his skirt burst into flame, the fire extinguisher put it out.

The music stopped, and Elvis disappeared in a cloud of fire retardant.

"At least he's gone," said Minnie.

Elvis stepped out of the smoke. "What was that for? I was just starting to get warmed up. Do you smell something burning?"

"It's getting late," said Moo. "We can come back and add up the scores later. I need a break!"

"I'm hungry," said Minnie. "What about Elvis?"

Moo crossed the stage and thanked Elvis for a stunning performance and then, while Elvis was looking for his bagpipes, she pulled the plug behind the amplifier.

"Brilliant! Come on," said Minnie.

They stepped off the stage, stopping to talk to some of the animals who had to leave early. Minnie made herself several sandwiches, using white bread on the outside and a double layer of chocolate and mayo on the inside.

Moo ate a banana.

The band played on, and the crowd danced into the night. After some time, the animals that lived on neighboring farms started to leave. A few who were sleeping over in the barn wandered off, yawning. Soon only the animals that lived on Red Tractor Farm with Minnie and Moo were left.

Irene and the band bundled up their musical instruments and then sat by the bonfire, talking late into the night.

Whenever the fire died down, someone would throw on a new log and sparks would rise up, adding more stars to an already glittering sky. The moon shone bright and clear, a crescent smile above them.

"We forgot the awards," said Moo.

"Oh, well," said Irene, standing up. "This way everyone is a winner. Good night."

"Good night," said Minnie.

"Good night," said Moo. "And thanks."

The band followed Irene as she walked off toward the barn.

The embers from the bonfire glowed, stirred by a cool breeze from the north. "Well?" said Moo, patting the money box. "What do you think?"

"Think? Moo, you know I have an allergy to thinking."

"I was just wondering what you thought about the festival."

"If I had to think, I'd say it was a night to remember. I liked it. I don't have to think about it to know it was fun for everyone. Everyone except maybe for the fox and his friends."

"You should sing more," said Moo.

Minnie put her arm around Moo. "What are you going to do about the money?"

"I thought I'd walk down to the farmhouse after everyone is gone and leave it."

"I hope you weren't planning on leaving the money in that old box? It's not very nice. It's rusty."

Moo nodded. "You're right. It's a gift. It should look pretty. How about one of those nice envelopes Mrs. Farmer is always throwing out after she reads the mail?"

"I saw some in the trash bins behind the house. You could use one of those."

"Perfect! I'll put it in the mailbox where they're sure to find it!"

Minnie and Moo sat quietly, listening to the crackling fire and the sounds of the October night.

Minnie started to say something but could tell Moo was lost somewhere in a place only Moo could go.

Moo stared into the last of the embers for the longest time. Then she looked up into the night, smiled to herself, and sighed.

Minnie sneezed.

20

The Farmer Returns

Mr. and Mrs. Farmer drove up to the farmhouse in their pickup truck and parked by the kitchen door.

The farmer stepped out of the truck and stretched.

"Ow!" he said, rubbing his back. He walked around the other side of the truck and opened the door for his wife, Millie.

"It's good to be home," said Millie.

"No place like it," John agreed.

Millie found the key under the mat and un-locked the kitchen door. John pulled the suitcases from the back of the truck and carried them into the house.

"I'll empty the suitcases," said Millie. "And throw the clothes into the wash. Shall I make lunch?"

"No hurry. How about a spot of tea for you and a cup of coffee for me?"

Millie put the kettle on the stove. "Good idea. I'll brew it up while you get the mail."

The farmer walked out to the mailbox. He stopped for a moment at the edge of the road and looked out over the farm. Not much had changed in the two weeks they were gone. There was a little more color in the trees, and the lawn needed mow-ing, but not much else.

"That's the way I like it," he thought. "Same

barn, same old broken-down tractor, same garden, same sheep grazing on the slope, same two cows staring at me from the top of the hill under the old oak tree.

"Yep, just the way I like it. Nice and quiet."

He removed the stack of letters crammed inside the mailbox, carried it back into the house, and put it on the kitchen table.

"Junk mail and bills," he said, sitting down. He slid a wastepaper basket out from under the table.

Millie handed John his coffee and sat down next to him with her cup of tea. "Anything interesting?"

"Nope, never is."

He sorted through the stack, tossing the junk mail into the wastebasket and putting the bills in a little pile in front of Millie.

"I suppose this pile is mine?"

The farmer laughed. "Yep!" he said. "And here's another one, a fat one from one of those contest mailings you're always getting. You know, the ones you always send a dollar to because you might win a million but never do!"

Millie shrugged. "You never know, John."

"Yes, I do. Here! It's all yours!"

Millie tore open the envelope and money exploded across the table and onto the floor.

"Oh! My goodness, John, I won! I won!"

"Oh my," said the farmer.

Other Minnie and Moo Books
by Denys Cazet

For Middle Readers:

Minnie & Moo
and the Seven Wonders of the World

For Beginning Readers:

Minnie & Moo
Go to the Moon
Go Dancing
Go to Paris
Save the Earth
The Thanksgiving Tree
The Musk of Zorro
Meet Frankenswine
The Potato From Planet X
The Night Before Christmas
Will You Be My Valentine?
Night of the Living Bed
Attack of the Easter Bunnies
The Case of the Missing Jelly Donut
Wanted: Dead or Alive
The Haunted Sweater

Elvis Rooster

Almost Goes to Heaven
The Magic Words

Remember, boys and girls, if you choose to ride your motorcycle through the playground, across the principal's front lawn, or down the aisle of a Walmart store, always wear proper clothing and always, always wear a helmet! Remember!

Safety First!

Denys Cazet is the author and illustrator of more than 50 picture books for children, including *Never Spit On Your Shoes,* winner of the California Young Readers Medal.

The books about Minnie and Moo started as early readers. They proved so popular, the series ran for fourteen titles. Then the two cows grew up and were featured in longer chapter books. *Hooves of Fire* is their second chapter book appearance.

Mr. Cazet was an elementary school teacher for 25 years, and has also been a school librarian and elementary school media specialist. He remains active in his local elementary school parent and advisory committees. A California native, Mr. Cazet lives with his wife and sons in the foothills of the Napa Valley where he also dabbles in the local sport of wine-making.